Out On a Limb

Hecate's Touch, Volume 1

Luis Paredes

Published by Platypus Book Press, 2023.

This is a work of fiction. Similarities to real people, places, or events are entirely coincidental.

OUT ON A LIMB

First edition. March 11, 2023.

Copyright © 2023 Luis Paredes.

ISBN: 979-8215119587

Written by Luis Paredes.

Dedicated to Rachel O'Donnell and her bunny, Bob.

Chapter One
The Legs

"How many perverts d'ya think sucked on those toes before the police rolled in?"

Rebecca Suarez groaned. She could always count on her partner, Peyton Marx, to class up a crime scene.

"Becca, seriously, how many?"

Rebecca cocked her head to the side, raised a sharp, black eyebrow, and considered the question. She stopped when her mind conjured a litter of unshaven, pot-bellied men suckling at the dangling digits.

"Christ! Peyton, why would you put that image in my mind?"

"Well, look how hard some of the guys in this crowd are staring at 'em. They're licking their lips." Peyton cast a nervous look around the group and lowered her voice. "I mean, I kinda get it. There is something erotic about how they hang."

She's not wrong, Rebecca thought, catching a glimpse of the pale flesh through the teeming crowd.

"Ugh, that's enough from you. Come on, I want to get closer and soak in some more details before we clock in." Rebecca shouldered her way through the mass of onlookers.

As people stepped aside, Rebecca and Peyton got their first unobstructed view of the crime scene: a tall oak tree, bristling with human legs.

The appendages sprouted seamlessly from the thick trunk, spiraling down from the canopy toward a square patch of dirt on the street below. Sneakers, high heels, sandals, and shreds of fabric littered the sidewalk alongside bright-orange evidence markers.

It seemed like half of Flushing, Queens stood gawking at the tree. Three police officers and a strip of flapping orange caution tape surrounding the scene barely held back the growing crowd.

No wonder Captain Wyatt had called her and Peyton in to consult. Unexplained Paranormal Phenomena, UPPs, were their specialty as Private Occult Investigators.

Despite the gruesome nature of the scene, Rebecca felt right at home. This wasn't even the most disturbing assignment the captain called her to consult on. That honor went to the children's birthday party at an Upper West Side apartment where a serial killer decorated the playroom with balloons made from the skin of his young victims' still-screaming faces.

Rebecca shuddered at the memory. Too many of the wrong kinds of people had been gifted powers since the Awakening, the day magic seeped into the world ten years ago when a six foot tall marble statue of the goddess Hecate walked out of a museum in Greece. Cell phone videos from that day showed the goddess lumbering through Athens toward the sea, leaving behind chunks of marble and clouds of iridescent purple dust in her wake. By the time Hecate made it to the port, she was just a pair of cracked legs standing ankle-deep in the Aegean.

Months later, thousands of people and a sliver of the animal population around the world discovered they'd been gifted with magical abilities. Most people think it was some kind of virus in the dust—the purple dust that wafted around the world, barely visible, except in the early morning light.

Conspiracy theorists, scientists, and theologians loved theorizing on how this happened, and how a marble statue could walk out of the museum, but the truth is no one knows a damn thing. The only thing the world agreed on was naming this ongoing phenomenon—Hecate's Touch.

People like Rebecca, who were already steeped in occult knowledge and powered by that magical spark, came into high demand in cities like New York where criminals started using spells, charms, and the occasional demon familiar to pull off fantastic crimes.

Someone nearby laughed. Rebecca turned her attention back toward the tree. She sighed as the youngest cop posed for a selfie with the gams in the background.

At least the ranking officer had the decency to break up the impromptu photoshoot, but now the older man was staring at Rebecca's chest. They *always* stared at her chest when she was with Peyton. It didn't help that she carried her partner like a baby on assignments.

At ten pounds, Peyton Marx was an abnormally large, caramel-colored Holland Lop rabbit. Intelligent, fast, and gifted with a sharp tongue, Peyton was a *Loquizoa*, one of the many animals born into the world after the Awakening with powers and the ability to talk.

"Becca, are we going in or what?" Peyton's dark-orange nose twitched as she sniffed the air. "I smell clues!"

A gaggle of onlookers turned and stared at Peyton.

Rebecca groaned. Pretty soon, they'd be asking to pet her partner. There were only 100 *Loquizoa* registered in New York City, so chances were high that most people in the crowd had never seen someone like Peyton up close. Smartphone cameras flickered to life and the crowd started to whisper excitedly among themselves.

"Ignore them." Rebecca said. She swaddled Peyton tighter. "Let's focus on what the officers are saying. Be a dear and lend me your ears, please."

Peyton grunted.

"I know I've been leaning on your sensory sharing skills a bit—"

Peyton's long whiskers twitched. "A bit, she says!"

Rebecca dragged a palm down her face. "Ok, a lot. I've been asking a lot of you lately, but it's not like we can afford expensive surveillance gadgets."

"Fine, but the captain's going to think we're wasting his time hovering," Peyton said, twitching her long, floppy ears. Instantly, Rebecca's hearing filtered out the chattering crowd and tuned to the officers' conversation:

"Sarge, how long until that Sigil Scanner gets here?"

"Anytime now, Cole. Dispatch says the machine is on its way from Long Island City. The captain called and said we're getting some extra help."

"For crowd control?"

"No, man, for the legs! Some kind of voodoo experts."

"Shit. I think it's just some kind of incantation gone wrong."

Peyton shook her head, severing their audio link. "Is that enough?"

"Yeah, yeah. I just need a snack before we start." Rebecca placed her partner on the concrete. She reached into the waist pocket of her oxblood-colored leather jacket and pulled out a plastic snack bag stuffed with olives.

"God, I wish you could lay off those things. I hate the smell," Peyton said, casting a disapproving glance at the oil stains mottling her partner's clothing.

"But they're delicious! Besides, you know that I need them," Rebecca said, picking a bulbous Agrinion from the mix.

"All that brine can't be good for your brain."

No, but they're great for keeping my powers in balance.

Olive trees were the only botanical species touched by Hecate, imbuing their fruit with traces of the goddess's magic. Mages fed on olives or sipped the oil to replenish their strength after casting spells.

Without a steady diet of olives, most mages weakened and suffered migraines, mood swings, stomach pains, and brain fog for days.

They were the lucky ones, Rebecca thought.

She dealt with the same symptoms *plus* a buildup of power in her system. If left unchecked—or provoked by fear or stress—the excess energy exploded from her body as dangerous plasma blasts. It had happened only once before. Luckily, Peyton wasn't near her at the time.

"You know, just because *Loquizoa* don't need olives to stay magically fit, doesn't mean you get to hate on them." Rebecca popped the glistening olive into her mouth. "Remember the last time I got *hangry?*"

"Ugh, don't remind me," Peyton said, shaking a drop of olive oil from her cheek.

"Are you two done?" a deep, resonant voice asked. The duo turned and looked up at Captain Miles Wyatt's scowling face—as usual, he wasn't happy.

"When I hire Suarez and Marx Investigators to consult on a crime scene, I expect the company's two founders to be in there and not out here, mingling with the civilians." He walked past and pulled the tape upward, motioning for them to walk through the yellow arch.

Standing on her hind legs, Peyton paddled the air with her stubby front feet.

Rebecca bent down and pressed her forehead against Peyton's quivering nose.

"Sorry, hun," Rebecca whispered. "You were right, I shouldn't have hovered."

"Gentleman, these are private detectives Suarez and Marx," Captain Wyatt said to the trio of officers as Rebecca made her way through with Peyton. Two of officers nodded while the youngest, the photogenic one, laughed. "A rabbit? That rabbit's a PI?"

"Cole, don't—" Captain Wyatt growled, pinching the bridge of his nose.

The rookie walked toward Peyton with a wriggling finger. "Can I pet it?"

Rebecca gasped and turned her body away, knowing how angry her partner could get in situations like this. Peyton had bit off a digit before. The lawsuit that followed almost bankrupted their business.

"No, you cannot pet me and I'm not an *it*," Peyton snapped, narrowing her round eyes to slits. "I'm *Loquizoa*. I've got rights—remember the 28th amendment?"

"Holy fuck! She can talk!" Cole shrieked, stumbling backward.

"Yeah, dummy. I can talk. Jesus Christ, these first-years," Peyton said, adding a snort to the end of her outburst. Rebecca squeezed her partner's warm, back foot and smiled, thankful Peyton's outburst was so tame this time around.

"Enough. All of you. Let's go over the scene with the PIs, please," Captain Wyatt said. "The department pays them good money to solve. . ." The captain waved his hands toward the legs. ". . .whatever this is. Sergeant, can you walk us through the crime scene?"

Chapter Two
Gathering Clues

The debriefing didn't take long.

Rebecca had gleaned most of the details the Sergeant rattled off from her observations behind the tape. But one detail stood out: all the wallets and purses found around the tree, presumably belonging to the victims, were emptied of cash and coin. Two officers and several bystanders also reported money stolen soon after arriving at the crime scene.

The empty billfolds might just be simple theft—an opportunistic pickpocket taking advantage while the cops secured the area. More likely, Rebecca thought, whatever spell caused this tree's transformation was still active. Rebecca's mind turned over the possibilities as the Sergeant's voice faded into the background:

". . .no fingerprints or sigils. That's why the captain called the PIs in...we think the bodies are still inside the tree. . ."

A fluttering shape in the tree drew Rebecca's attention upward. A bright-red cardinal hopped around the leafless canopy and settled on the stub of a freshly cut branch near the power lines.

Peyton padded up her partner's shoulder. Her moist, black eyes quivered with excitement. "I see it, too. If I were to do anything funny to this tree, that's exactly where I'd do it from."

"Me too, and I bet this happened recently." Rebecca squatted to her haunches. She dabbed her fingers on a thin coat of sawdust dusting covering the tree's exposed roots.

"Maybe Cole was right," Rebecca said, not expecting anyone but Peyton to hear.

"Right about what?" the captain asked.

"I overhead Cole earlier saying that this could be an incantation gone wrong," Rebecca said. "There have been cases of spells backfiring."

"Do you think that's what happened here?" the captain asked.

"I don't know about that, but I'm sure we'll be able to find out who did this by looking up there," Rebecca said, pointing toward the freshly cut stumps near the crown of the tree. "The only people who could cast without attracting attention with so many people walking about are the arborists who pruned this oak."

"But why would they cast the spell so high up?" Cole asked.

Peyton wriggled out of Rebecca's arms and hopped toward the young officer.

"Incantations and spells imprint a mage's personal sigil on the object or person the magic's working on, riiiiiight?" Peyton narrowed her eyes at Cole.

The rookie pouted.

"And every sigil is as unique as a fingerprint. So, whoever did this would want to hide their mark for as long as possible."

Rebecca's heart swelled with pride. Peyton's occult knowledge surpassed her own and she loved seeing her partner school the patrolman.

"Are we losing you, Cole?" Rebecca asked.

"No. No, you're not. I know that. *Everyone* knows that," Cole snapped, puffing his chest. "Once that Sigil Scanner gets here, we'll scan the tree, but it's not here yet."

"Well, we don't have to wait. We have Peyton," Rebecca said, finger-gunning toward her partner.

Cole rubbed his head. "I don't get it."

"I can see sigils without any fancy equipment. All *Loquizoa* can see 'em," Peyton said.

"You'll need a lift though," Rebecca said, tying her black hair into a ponytail.

Peyton nodded and hopped back toward her partner's black sneakers.

Everyone watched as Peyton planted her front paws and stretched her rear legs.

A collective "aww" rose from the crowd.

"Fucking humans," Peyton said, scratching the side of her puffy cheeks with a back paw. "C'mon, Becca, let's fly."

Rebecca shut her eyes and chanted, "*Ánodos, ánodos, ánodos!*" Strands of purple electricity erupted from her back and shaped themselves into bat wings.

"Jesus Christ!" Cole shrieked. He covered his eyes as the translucent wings flapped in place, spreading lavender sparks into the air. The crowd oohed and aahed while surging backward.

The captain whipped out a pair of sunglasses from his front pocket and set them over his eyes. "Those two are a pain in the ass, but I love watching them work."

"What's she saying?" the rookie asked.

"*Ánodos* means, to rise," the captain said. He jutted his chin toward Peyton. "Just watch."

The air crackled with static as Peyton levitated a few feet above the ground.

Rebecca grinned, sensing Cole's discomfort. The rookie would pee his pants if he saw what she could really do. Incantations were nothing compared to her other skills—energy manipulation, divination, mind control, bodily possession, astral projection—she could even warp the space around her body, letting objects and projectiles pass through harmlessly.

The only talent she lacked was necromancy. Only a handful of people were touched with the power to raise the dead and channel the strange energies of corpses. They never lasted long; necromages barely survived past their late teens. Rebecca clenched her eyes tighter. Maybe some types of magic were like cancer?

No! Don't go there! Rebecca shook the idea away. But the thought lingered, oozing through her brain until Peyton yelled, "Look, up in the sky! Faster than a speeding carrot!"

She opened her eyes. Peyton hovered in a Superman pose, her long ears slicked back. Rebecca laughed, grateful for the distraction.

"I'll take it from here, Becca," Peyton said, flattening out her body.

With Peyton fully charged by the levitation spell, she reached into her pocket and plucked out a fresh olive. Her wings slowly faded away as she chewed on a few more of the salty treats.

Peyton paddled the air with her front paws to gain altitude, rising to the canopy. From there, she maneuvered around the branches in a descending spiral, using her stiff tail and bowed, back legs like a rudder to angle around the tree limbs and dangling human legs. Halfway down, she spotted a clue.

"I see something, Becca! It's definitely someone's mark, but. . .it's changing."

"Changing? How?"

"It's morphing as I'm staring at it. The lines are twisting themselves into new shapes."

"Can I see?"

"No problem." Peyton gestured the shape of a circle with her right front foot, etching a bright, neon-blue line onto the air. "One order of sensory sharing coming right up!"

Peyton hovered backward and spat. Her saliva hit an invisible wall at the hoop's center and oozed toward the outer edges like soap scum.

A thin layer of milk-white mucus spread across Rebecca's eyes.

Cole covered his mouth and gagged. "What the hell?"

"Not all magic's pretty, Cole." Rebecca rubbed her temples. The cloudy film evaporated, and she saw the sigil through her partner's eyes.

Peyton was right. Every few seconds, the sigil twisted itself into a new symbol—four to be precise.

This is getting good! Rebecca rubbed her hands together. Sigils were fixed, unalterable. The strange, twisting rune in front of her was proof that they were dealing with someone—or something—powerfully new.

"Cole, you'll want to get that Sigil Scanner down here soon. Peyton's right, this sigil's special." Rebecca shook her head to restore her own vision.

"Not a problem. It just got here," the rookie said.

He stepped aside for two blond police technicians wearing lab coats. They rolled in a stout metal box the size of a dishwasher with a black, glass dome on top.

"Wow, that's an old one!" Rebecca said, walking around the scanner and admiring the evil eye painted on all four sides. The thick, concentric circles of dark blue, teal, and white surrounding a black bull's eye made for a mesmerizing design.

"It's got Wi-Fi," the male tech said, giving the scanner a reassuring tap on the dome.

"And connects by Bluetooth," added the woman holding a computer tablet. She extended a hand. "I'm Mabel by the way. And that's my brother, Cain. So, what are we scanning? The legs or the tree?"

Peyton floated down to the twins and pointed out where the sigil was etched into the oak. "The signature changes every few seconds."

"There are four distinct symbols," Rebecca added.

"Not a problem." Mabel tapped her tablet and smiled. "I've programmed the scanner to take a few snapshots."

The box whirred to life and a series of flashes blew out from the dome, bathing the scene in crisp, white light. Seconds later, the four sigils Rebecca and Peyton saw appeared on the technician's screen.

"They look rough, but more than enough to run through the database," Cain said, looking over Mabel's shoulder at the images.

Peyton landed on the concrete and turned to Rebecca. "How long you think it'll take 'em to—"

"Got them!" Mabel shouted. "The sigils match up to Dakota Wells, Finley Aubrey, Kit Martinez, and Quinn Meyers. I don't have much more than their names." Mabel tapped the screen. "Database is slow today."

"Well, we can assume that at least one of those ladies is a mage powerful enough to cast this tree spell," Rebecca said. "Where can we find them?"

"Wait, what makes you think they're women?" Cole asked.

Rebecca shook her head. "Who else would be powerful enough to cast a spell like this?" She caught Mabel rolling her eyes at Cole. "See? She gets it. Now, where can we find our suspects?"

"Says here that all four work at Emerald Tree Care in Forest Hills." Mabel stared up at the dangling legs.

"Forest Hills. Sounds fancy. That's probably all the way up in Westchester, right?" Peyton asked.

Captain Wyatt scoffed. "No, it's here in Queens."

Peyton groaned and scratched the side of her head with her rear paw. "Oh, my gawd! I don't want to take the bus! I get motion sickness on those smelly things."

"Don't be so dramatic. I'm sure we can get a ride," Rebecca said. She glanced over to the captain. "We can ride with you, right?"

"Sure. Right after the techs print out what I need," Captain Wyatt said.

Mabel nodded and tapped the tablet. A high-pitched screech filled the air. The Sigil Scanner rocked back and forth as a sheet of paper slowly inched out of a thin slit in front of the machine.

The captain ripped the page out and tore off the strips of perforated edging. "This provisional warrant gives us the authority to interrogate the suspects based on—"

SNIP!

The sound cut through the conversation and everyone under the tree turned to face a short, elderly woman in a sharp, black business suit. She held a pair of oversized scissors in one hand and a business card in the other. The severed caution tape slithered around her thin ankles and settled in a coiled mass around her shoes.

"Who the fuck are you?" the captain asked.

Chapter Three
Incantation Spreads

"Nily Ann Liu, President of the Flushing Business Association," the woman said, pausing to see if her name and title made an impression.

Rebecca rolled her eyes as Peyton hopped to her side.

Undeterred, Nily tucked her business card into the captain's shirt pocket and patted it in place. Her eyes darted between the legs in the tree, the Sigil Scanner, the captain, and back to the legs.

"How much longer do you plan on keeping this intersection closed? It's one of the busiest sections on Main Street and my constituents are losing money by the minute." She waved her scissors in the air.

"Ma'am, there's been a serious thaumaturgical incident here," the captain said, gesturing toward the legs. "As you can see, we have no idea how to move the bodies yet. And you know what? You're not supposed to be here. I'm going to need you to step away and—"

"Can't you just chop them off?"

The captain's faced twisted in disbelief. "Excuse me?"

"Chop. Them. Off," Nily repeated, slowly.

"Seriously? Mrs. Liu, come on!" Rebecca gestured toward the legs. "Just look at what happened here! How can you be worried about money when all these people have died?"

Rebecca flinched as Nily pointed the scissors at her chest. "Oh, I've heard of you two. Suarez and Marx, is it? You and your little pet there always leave behind a trail of bodies. I remember how that incident on Kissena Boulevard turned out last year."

"Hey, that wasn't our fault. That demon was suicidal. How were we supposed to know he rigged himself with explosives," Peyton said.

As Nily opened her mouth to respond, a high-pitched scream filled the air.

"That wasn't me," she whispered, dropping the scissors.

The police, Rebecca, Peyton, and even the chattering crowd surrounding the crime scene froze and looked around. The cars on Main Street slowed to a crawl as the screaming intensified.

"Mom! MOMMA!!"

Rebecca ran toward the voice. Captain Wyatt and the three officers followed closely behind. Halfway down the street, they found the source of the yelling. The sight curdled their stomachs—a little girl straining to pull her mother's head out of an elm tree.

"Momma! Momma!" the girl cried, pulling at the bark where her mother's neck joined the tree.

All Rebecca and Peyton could do was watch. More shouts and screams filled the air. Across the street, a jogger grasped at roots coiling around her ankle and a man gurgled blood as sharp branches stabbed his neck.

"Everyone off the streets!" Rebecca yelled. "Get inside and stay away from the trees!" She pulled the nearest officer by the collar. "You! Get on a bullhorn and start evacuating Main Street. No one's safe here!"

The patrolman nodded and ran off.

"Becca, I think it's time we get the hell out of here too," Peyton said.

"Right." Rebecca turned, tripping over a panicked shopper and Peyton rolled out of her arms, landing inches from the tree that swallowed the little girl's mother.

Rebecca stared into Peyton's quivering eyes, and whispered, "Run."

Peyton darted into Rebecca's arms just as a spear-shaped branch stabbed the concrete and shattered into splinters.

"That was too close," Rebecca said, hugging her partner close.

Peyton snuggled into Rebecca's shoulder. "Yeah, let's not do that again."

"No guarantees with this job." Rebecca stood and watched as the trees snatched victims with their writhing limbs. She took a step toward the crosswalk as a police cruiser squealed to a stop.

"Get in, you two!" Captain Wyatt yelled. "We're going to Forest Hills!"

Chapter Four
Emerald Tree Care

Rebecca stroked Peyton's trembling back as Captain Wyatt inched through traffic. The soft, tawny fur flattened, then flared as her hand glided back and forth. The motion calmed Rebecca's nerves, but Peyton's tiny heart thumped hard and fast. *Poor girl.*

They had some close calls, but this one felt worse somehow. Rebecca shook her head. She didn't want to imagine a life without her best friend and partner. Peyton hopped into her life nine years ago, just a year after losing her seven-year-old daughter, Claire, to leukemia.

The Awakening had just touched Rebecca, and she was living through a roller-coaster of emotions when she found a brick-sized baby Peyton rooting through their tiny backyard vegetable garden. She had laughed, for the first time in weeks, at the tiny, furry rump rustling through a row of salad greens.

"And who's this little thief?" she had asked not expecting an answer. Hardly anyone at that time, including Rebecca, had heard of *Loquizoa*. She stumbled backward as Peyton snapped her head around, belched, and started talking.

"Lady, you should be paying me to eat these scrawny veggies!"

Rebecca watched, dumbfounded, as Peyton pawed at a wilted green shoot and pulled out what looked like a small blood clot. "Seriously, you call this thing a radish?"

And just like that, Peyton stole her heart. Rebecca invited her future partner into her home, and they'd been together ever since. Peyton, like all *Loquizoa*, developed faster than humans and was eager to learn all about Rebecca's obsession—the occult. She read every book in Rebecca's personal library and devoured any scrap of text related to magic. Two years after they met, they solved their first case and opened shop as private investigators.

Rebecca smiled at the memory and pressed her head against the passenger side window; her breath plumed on the glass and evaporated. Her eyes fluttered closed.

"You two almost died out there," Officer Cole said.

The rookie had made it into the car. Rebecca was so addled by the murderous trees that she didn't even look in the back seat.

Rebecca turned around and glared.

"What? I jumped in the car before you guys." Cole clutched the seatbelt across his chest.

"I couldn't stop him," the captain grumbled.

"Sir, with all due respect, I was right about the incantation going wrong," Cole said, meeting the captain's stare in the rearview mirror. "I want to see this through."

Rebecca nodded, admiring Cole's plucky determination. He seemed to be just as invested in the case as she was.

"You should wake Peyton up. We're here," the captain said, turning the car onto the gravel covered parking lot of Emerald Tree Care.

The arborist's headquarters was a simple, two-story, cinderblock building. Patches of algae and black mold mottled the white stucco. Rusted, green metal letters spelled out the company's name above the glass double doors.

Rebecca stepped out of the cruiser and cracked her back. "This place has seen better days."

"Yikes! It makes our dumpy studio office look like paradise," Peyton said, hopping from the passenger side window and into her partner's arms.

The captain slammed his door shut and walked toward the building.

Cole adjusted his patrol hat and stretched his arms. "Captain wants you to follow him," Cole said.

Peyton rolled her eyes. "No shit, rookie."

As they walked, Rebecca eyed the bucket trucks in the parking lot. Any one of those could have helped a mage reach a tree's canopy and work her incantation. All except the half dozen trucks resting on cinder blocks.

A little boy sat inside one of the disabled vehicles. He hopped out as Rebecca walked past and joined their march toward the building. He walked to Rebecca's right, shuffling his bare feet through the coarse stone.

Kid must have inch-thick soles, Rebecca thought, glancing at the child. She guessed he was about six or seven. He was skinny, but seemed healthy, strong. His sinewy, tanned arms swung back and forth as he walked. Splotches of dried grape jelly stained his cheeks and the oversized Star Wars tank top he wore.

The boy looked up and met her stare. Cold, blue eyes peeked through a curtain of thin, blond hair. Rebecca's heart skipped. His round, youthful face was etched with wrinkles! The creases weren't deep and almost faded from view as the sunlight danced on his skin. The boy's thin lips parted. Laugh lines darted from the edges of his nostrils and into the curl of his sneering lips.

"I like your coat. It looks like its covered in blood," he said. His voice was flat and raspy.

Beads of sweat bloomed on Rebecca's back. "Um, thanks. Are you coming in too?" She asked, forcing a smile.

The boy stopped walking, stuck his tongue out, and blew a raspberry.

"What a weirdo," Peyton said.

"You're a weirdo!" the boy shot back.

Rebecca jiggled Peyton in her arms. "Calm down, I don't think he really means it."

The sound of hinges squeaking turned Rebecca's attention as Captain Wyatt opened the glass doors. The little boy barreled inside, clucking and flapping his arms like a chicken.

Was Claire ever that strange? Rebecca shook her head. The oddest thing her daughter ever did was pretend she was a cat and *that* was adorable.

"Alright, the kid's weird," Rebecca said. "Let's catch up."

She followed Captain Wyatt and Cole into the main office. The receptionist sitting at a stout oak table stood up and smiled. "Hello, are you officers looking for a career change?"

Captain Wyatt chuckled and flashed his badge. "No, ma'am. I'm Captain Miles Wyatt. Behind me is Officer Cole and Private Occult Investigators Rebecca Suarez and Peyton Marx. We're here—"

"The bunny?" Alma asked.

Peyton growled.

"Yes, Inspector Marx is *Loquizoa*, but that's not important," the captain said, removing his hat. "We really need to speak to the owner. It's urgent."

"No problem, you're talking to her. I'm Alma Hill, and I run Emerald Tree Care along with my husband, Jacob." Alma narrowed her eyes. "What's this about?"

"Mrs. Hill, there's been a serious incident in Flushing where your company did some work last week."

Alma crossed her arms. "Really? What kind of incident."

"An incantation is making the trees attack people," Rebecca said.

Alma laughed. "What makes you think we had anything to do with something like that? We're arborists, not mages."

"You think this is funny?" Rebecca ran her hands through her hair. "I just watched a mother die in front of her child!"

Alma stepped around the desk and stood in front of Rebecca, inches from her face. Flecks of amber sparkled in the woman's frigid, blue eyes. "I'm sorry to hear. Like I said, we don't do any of that. . ." Alma waved an invisible baton in the air. ". . .magical stuff."

Rebecca wanted to punch the woman.

The captain tapped Rebecca's shoulder. "Why don't you take a step back, Saurez. Have an olive—or two."

Rebecca nodded and walked behind Cole. She'd let Captain Wyatt do the talking now.

"Our scanner found a sigil on an oak, and it matches four of your employees," the captain said.

Alma shook her head. "Th-that's impossible. A sigil's unique. How can one mark match four people?"

Rebecca eyes widened. Alma was nervous! She shouldered past Cole to get a better view of her facial reactions.

"The Sigil Scanner never fails," Captain Wyatt said. "Besides, Inspector Marx scanned the tree and saw the same symbols. Rebecca witnessed the same through sensory sharing."

Alma glared at Peyton. "You can do that?"

This bitch knows something!

"Yeah, sigil scanning's just one of my many talents." Peyton rubbed her right front foot against her chest. She stretched out her claws and blew on them. "I'm also a boss at astral projection, remote viewing, sensory sharing, and magical lock picking."

"Ok, right." Alma picked up the phone on her desk. "I think I should call my lawyer."

The captain whipped out a folded sheet of paper from his shirt pocket. "Be my guest, but we do have a provisional warrant."

Rebecca stepped forward. It was time to play good inspector. "Alma, please. It'll only take a few hours. Think of all the lives you could save," she said, softening her tone. "We just need a small space and—"

"Maaaahm!" a child whined. "You're talking too much! I can hear your words in my head again!"

It was the little boy from earlier. He wrapped himself around Alma's legs like a spider.

"I'm sorry. This is Charlie, my son. He's—"

"Mom! Stop talking!" Charlie said, squeezing his arms and legs tighter around her.

"Honey, please," Alma said, wrangling Charlie around the desk and into her office chair. She held her son in place and turned toward the group. "Charlie's an only child and grew up in the office. He thinks he's the boss."

"MOM!"

"Enough!" Alma snapped, pressing her head against Charlie's scalp. "Keep your ass in that seat and let the grown-ups talk."

The boy curled into a ball and whimpered. Alma adjusted her hair, smoothed out the wrinkles on her pants, and faced the captain.

"Why don't I call in my husband? He directs all the work crews," Alma pressed a button on the intercom.

"Jacob, please come to the front. There are cops here," Alma snarled. Her voice echoed throughout the building.

A lean, bald man ducked under the office door. When he straightened, his head was inches from the lobby ceiling. He wore a neon-orange jumpsuit and rubbed a cloth over the lenses of his thin wire-rimmed glasses.

"Whoa, did we just walk into an NBA draft? Look at this guy! He's gotta be at least—"

"Peyton!" Rebecca said. She looked up at Jacob. "I'm so sorry, Mr. Hill. My partner has no filter."

Peyton tried to squirm out of Rebecca's grasp.

Jacob laughed and adjusted his glasses. "It's not a problem. I'm used to all the tall jokes. How can I help you, officers?"

"They say the trees you worked on in Flushing have turned into monsters," Alma said.

Cole raised a finger. "That's not what the captain said. He said—"

"The pin oaks? Yeah, the Flushing Business Association hired us to prune them back. Their branches were too close to the power lines," Jacob said. "It was a simple line job. Alma even took Charlie to see the crew work. Did something go wrong?"

"Yes, something went wrong. The trees you clipped are eating people now!" Peyton yelled. "One of 'em nearly got me."

Jacob grunted. "What? And you think we had some something to do with it? I don't have a single mage on the payroll." He paused and looked at the captain and Cole. He held up his palms and stepped back. "Wait, wait, wait! This is because I hire folks with records, right? That's why you're bringing this shit to my doorstep? You want to pin this on one of my workers."

Alma rubbed Jacob's back. "Honey, we need to call our lawyer right now."

"Alma, Jacob, people are dying out there. The quicker we talk to your people, the quicker we can figure this out," Rebecca pleaded. "And the quicker we'll get out of your hair."

Jacob rubbed the stubble on his chin. He glanced at Alma and they both nodded. "Fine, I'll gather the folks you need and the activity logs from that day so you can see we're on the up and up here." He turned to his wife. "Alma, can you take them to the break room and let them set up there?"

"Thank you," Rebecca said.

Alma rolled her eyes and walked out the door.

Rebecca followed and reached into her coat pocket. Her fingers tapped the plastic ziplock and her stomach spasmed, realizing that there were only a few olives left.

"This isn't good," Rebecca whispered.

"What?" Peyton asked.

"I'm almost out of olives."

"Oh, Lord! This is going to get interesting."

Chapter Five
Interrogation Prep

Rebecca watched Peyton scamper across the long break room table. Her feet thumped and scratched along the edge, knocking over the captain's notepad and pencil.

"I fucking love interrogations!" Peyton yelled.

Where'd she get her energy? Rebecca envied her partner's carefree spirit. On most days, she'd let her partner do her thing, but today Rebecca's last few nerves were frayed to the breaking point and she was out of olives. She'd scarfed down the last handful as they walked toward the break room.

"Peyton!" Rebecca said through clenched teeth, "Act professional."

"I can't help it!" Peyton slid to a stop and faced Rebecca. "Thanks to the warrant in the cap's pocket, I can turn my Gaze on the four mooks Jacob's bringing in."

"Your Gaze? What's that? Some kind of *Loki-zo-uh* x-ray?" Cole asked, shifting in his metal chair.

"First off, that's not how you pronounce *Low-quee-zoh-ah*," Peyton said. "Second, it's nothing like an x-ray. The Gaze illuminates magical auras. Anyone that's been touched by Hecate has one."

"What do they look like?" Cole asked.

Peyton's whiskers quivered. "Clouds. They look like candy-colored vapor floating around a body. They vibrate too. And once the jiggling starts, thin tentacles spray out and tickle the air like sea anemones on steroids."

Cole's eyes widened. "Get out!"

"It's true," Rebecca said. "I've seen it through sensory sharing."

Cole shook his head. "Wait, what good does looking at an aura do? I thought we were here to interrogate these folks."

Captain Wyatt grunted. "Isn't Thaumaturgy 101 a required course at the academy, Cole?"

The young officer blushed. "Sorry, sir. It's just that it's all a lot to take in, and that was over a year ago."

"It's ok, Cap. I like schooling rookies," Peyton said. "An aural reading is going to tell me right away if any of these suspects were capable of casting that spell."

"It's the color of the aura that gives them away," Rebecca said. "Weak mages have sooty, gray auras that cling to the outline of their bodies. Folks that can cast spells and incantations have bright, colorful signatures."

Cole's head bobbed up and down. "Ah, ok."

"So, if any of these four have a dull aura, we can pretty much rule them out," Peyton said.

"Wouldn't it be wild if this was the work of a *Phytomagus*?" Rebecca asked. "We've never come across a mage with power over plants."

The break room door creaked opened. Jacob stooped under the door frame. "You guys ready?"

Peyton thumped her rear feet. "Let's get ready to rumble!"

The captain rolled his eyes. "Oh, for God's sake. Yes, please let them in."

Chapter Six
Unusual Suspects

"It's a sausage party," Rebecca muttered as the four suspects walked in.

She couldn't believe the colossal mistake she had made—Dakota, Finley, Kit, and Quinn were all men.

"Something wrong?" Cole asked.

Rebecca groaned. She jabbed a finger toward the four men. "All of these suspects are guys."

"What's wrong with that?" Cole asked.

"Everything!" Rebecca snapped.

How could Cole not understand? The Awakening didn't gift magic evenly across the human population. Women received the highest dosage and widest spectrum of powers. Most men touched by Hecate ended up as simple psychics or diviners. Only a small percentage could wield magic like a mage.

The captain rapped the table with his knuckles. "Well, out with it."

Rebecca's eyes widened. The captain couldn't be that ignorant, could he? Her heart raced as she struggled to compose herself. "Captain, it's just that most limp wands—"

Kit stepped forward and waved his arms. "Hey! You can't call us that!"

Fiery, red sparks ignited around Rebecca's head. Kit's eyes widened. Rebecca glared at the arborist. "Look, it's not my fault the goddess shortchanged you, you—"

"Inspector Suarez, please!" Captain Wyatt stood and faced the four arborists. "Gentlemen, on behalf of the NYPD, I'd like to apologize for our consultant's outburst."

Rebecca waved her hand across her face, extinguishing the tiny flares dancing in the air. She lost control again. The captain usually overlooked Rebecca's occasional slipup and Peyton's unprofessional outbursts, but she had crossed a line by using the derogatory term for male mages. Even Peyton glared at her.

"I'm sure that Inspector Suarez will continue with the utmost professionalism from here on out," the captain said. He turned to face Rebecca. "Isn't that right, Suarez?"

Rebecca placed her hands palm down on the desk and took in a deep breath. "Right. Sorry. What I meant to say was that the majority of, um, *touched* males aren't powerful enough to cast a spell like the one in Flushing."

Captain Wyatt sat back down. "Isn't it possible that two or more of our suspects here could have worked together?"

The Captain had a point. Individuals could form magical clusters to amplify their powers. She wondered if these four had the chutzpah and occult know-how to even perform that kind of ritual.

Peyton nuzzled Rebecca's hand with her nose. "Answer him," she whispered.

Rebecca wasn't used to being the one on the outs with her boss. The role reversal troubled her. She faced the captain. "Yes, sir. It's a possibility."

"Then, Inspector Marx, please proceed with your Gaze."

Peyton saluted the captain with the flick of her front foot, hopped to the center of the table, and crouched. The tips of her long almond-shaped ears kissed the tabletop, and her stubby, white tail rocked side to side.

"That's freaking adorable," Quinn said as the other three suspects chuckled.

"Yeah, yeah, yeah. I've heard it all before," Peyton growled. "Now, I need all of you to stay absolutely still, like you're posing for an old-timey, stagecoach photograph."

As the men composed themselves, a thin, clear membrane stretched across Peyton's eyes. Rebecca groaned and stumbled backward. Her vision clouded over.

"We've got some residual sensory sharing," Peyton said.

"Yeah, it happens," Rebecca muttered, steadying herself. She blinked and rubbed her eyes with the heels of her hands. Slowly, she saw the room through Peyton's vision. It was disorienting. Her body stood rooted in one spot, but her eyesight drank the world in from an entirely different position.

Worse still, the Gaze filtered light, leached colors, and reversed darks and lights, giving the world the look of a film negative.

Rebecca's heart skipped as puffs of gray smoke bellowed out from behind the four men. The clouds roiled around their bodies like smoke caught in a glass tube.

She watched as Peyton stood on her hind legs and glanced down at her furry feet. An orange haze pulsing with veins of red electricity warbled around her partner's body. The difference between the emanations was jarring.

"What's the verdict?" The captain asked.

Rebecca knew the answer, but she let Peyton answer.

"Bupkis, Cap. Even if all four of these guys formed a cluster, they wouldn't be able to turn on a lightbulb."

Kit stepped forward. "Hey, that's not fair. I can levitate things." He paused. "Small objects. Coins and stuff."

Peyton rolled her eyes. "That's nice, but we're looking for someone a bit more—"

"Ba-BOK!"

Rebecca and Peyton flinched as Charlie barreled through the door clucking like a chicken. Strands of purple energy trailed from the boy's body like flames.

Rebecca couldn't believe it. There were plenty of children touched by Hecate in the past few years, but they grew into their powers. A child Charlie's age should have had a lightly colored aura, not this wild and fiery plumage.

"Peyton, please tell me I'm not the only one seeing this?" Rebecca asked.

Peyton's fur bristled as the purple filaments spread throughout the room. "Oh, I'm seeing it. This kid's aural signature is just as powerful as yours, Becca. Maybe stronger."

Charlie turned and yelled. The boy's screech severed the sensory sharing link between Rebecca and Peyton.

Jacob rushed into the room and scooped Charlie into his arms. "Sorry about that."

Charlie slipped out of his father's grip and pointed at Peyton. "Dad! The bunny looked at me funny!"

Jacob's head snapped toward Peyton. "Did you scan my son?"

Peyton nodded. "It was an accident. He ran into my field of view. I couldn't—"

"You had no right to do that!"

Captain Wyatt stood. "You're absolutely correct, Mr. Hill. Inspector Marx was—"

"Way out of line, that's what!" Jacob shouted. "I should call my lawyer right now."

Peyton hopped into Rebecca's lap as Jacob turned his anger toward the captain.

"Christ on a stick, girl. How did Charlie snap you out of your Gaze and break our link?" Rebecca asked.

"I don't know, but I felt the kid in my mind."

Rebecca shook her head. "That's impossible."

Peyton nuzzled into her partner's shoulder. "Becca, I'm scared. That kid's creepy as hell."

Rebecca glanced up. "Shh. Not so loud. I think he heard you."

Charlie wrestled out of his father's arms and stomped toward Rebecca and Peyton. His sweaty feet slapped against the concrete floor.

"I know people think I'm creepy," Charlie said. The crinkles radiating out from his eyelids deepened. "It's not my fault I look like this. Bunnies look kinda funny too. They eat their own poop. Did you know that?"

Peyton gasped. "You take that back!"

"Calm down, Peyton," Rebecca said, trying to hold her squirming friend in place.

"Let me go, Becca! Just one bite and I'll set him—"

Rebecca wrapped her arms around Peyton's head. Her muffled threats pressed against Rebecca's jacket. Jacob picked Charlie up and patted his back. The boy whimpered and drooped over his father's shoulders. Charlie grinned and stuck his tongue out at Rebecca.

"Ok, my turn to apologize," Jacob said.

Rebecca glared at Jacob. The man didn't know he was being played by his son, or he chose to ignore the boy's manipulative behavior. Either way, it wasn't the time or place to say anything about the man's parenting skills.

Charlie whined again as his father talked. "My boy wasn't trying to be mean. He's got no filter and just says things. . .bluntly."

"Yeah, I know what that's like," Rebecca said.

"Let's just forget this happened," Jacob said. He turned his body so that Charlie could see Peyton. "Can you apologize to the inspector?"

"No," Charlie muttered.

Peyton's muzzle wriggled from between Rebecca's arms. The slits in her nose widened and narrowed rapidly. "Whatever."

"Just make sure you leave anything related to my son out of your reports." He turned toward Captain Wyatt. "Can my crew get back to work?"

"Yes. We're done here. Thank you for all your help," the captain said, handing Jacob a business card. "Please call me if anything strange happens with the trees in this neighborhood."

"But, Captain—" Peyton started to say.

The captain snapped his pencil in half and tossed the splintered halves into a metal trash bin at the corner of the room. "Pack it up, Marx. You and Suarez are finished."

Chapter Seven
Repercussions

Rebecca scrolled through her bank's smartphone app as she followed Captain Wyatt and Cole out the door. Her eyes widened at the sight of their account's minuscule balance.

There was just enough cash in checking to cover expenses this week and a tiny safety net in savings that could, with some serious penny pinching, get them through the month. Maybe.

If they were "finished," as the captain had growled, then Suarez and Marx Investigators, LLC was as good as dead; their retainer with the NYPD accounted for more than half their monthly revenue.

Sweat beaded across her forehead as she imagined their landlord pasting an eviction sticker on their apartment door. Rebecca squeezed Peyton closer to her chest.

"Rent's gonna be a bitch next month," her partner said.

"You psychic now?"

Floppy ears slapped Rebecca's chest as Peyton shook her head. "No, but I'm pretty sure you're thinking the same thing."

"Yeah, what's that?"

Peyton puffed out her furry cheeks. "We're screwed."

Rebecca slowed her pace and let Captain Wyatt and Cole walk ahead. She rubbed Peyton's furry head. "I fucked up. I shouldn't have called those guys limp wands."

"It's ok. It wasn't just you. I told a little boy that I'd bite him." Peyton nuzzled into Rebecca's chest. "Hey, no matter what happens, we'll work it out. I can always switch to a low-carb hay diet. I can stand to lose a few pounds and your back will thank me."

Rebecca nodded, but she thought of their bank balance again.

The captain cleared his throat. "You two know that I can always hear you, right?"

"Sorry, Captain," Rebecca said, jogging toward the cruiser.

"Don't worry, you two aren't fired. . .yet." Captain Wyatt tapped the car's roof. "Now get in. I want to talk about what happened."

Rebecca closed the door and let Peyton settle into her lap. She stretched the seat belt over and clicked it into place. Captain Wyatt put the car in reverse and backed out of the parking lot.

"Now, before the two of you say anything, I need to make something very clear," the captain said, turning onto the main road. "Suarez, you need to work on that temper. And Marx, you need to get that mouth of yours under control. Is that understood?"

Rebecca and Peyton nodded.

"Good. Now we can move forward. I heard what you two said in the break room. Jacob's son is powerful, isn't he?"

Peyton's head snapped up. "Yeah, freakishly so. I've never seen an aura like that on anyone besides Rebecca or that bayou witch, Metis Black, we met in Louisiana last year. They're about the same age and hardly anyone post-Awakening's been touched like my girl or Metis."

Rebecca stood a little straighter. She was proud of her magical abilities. And Peyton made a good point: Hecate's Touch continued its march across the world, but the phenomena's strength waned over the years. But maybe Charlie was proof that the Goddess's power was making a comeback, and the boy was just a preview of what was to come?

Captain Wyatt grunted. "Do you think Charlie's somehow behind all of this?"

"I guess he could be, but why? There's no motive." Rebecca said. "Why would a kid do that? Just to hurt people?"

"What about the parents?"

"I got a weird vibe from Alma," Rebecca said.

"Me too," Peyton added.

"When Jacob scooped up his kid, did you catch a glimpse of his aura?"

Peyton shook her head. "Nah, he doesn't have any powers."

The captain nodded. "It'd be helpful to turn your Gaze on the mother and scan the kid again. I want to know what they're really capable of."

"How?" Peyton asked. "We don't have a warrant for those two."

"Well, there's nothing that says you can't scan them out in public. We could, hypothetically, park across the street from their offices and wait for them to drive by," the captain mused. "Whatever you see wouldn't be admissible in court, but it could help us out. Besides, it's already five in the afternoon. If we head back now, we'll catch them at quitting time."

"Say no more, Cap! I love a good stakeout!" Peyton said.

Chapter Eight
Stakeout

Rebecca hated stakeouts.

Patrol cars weren't built with comfort in mind and the passenger seat she'd been squirming on for the past five hours felt as if it was cast from concrete.

The lack of creature comforts, however, hadn't stopped the captain or Cole from drifting off to sleep.

Peyton sucked in a breath of air through her long teeth. One of her eyes widened while the other squeezed shut. "Can you believe our luck? The cap parks us behind this stinking dumpster so I can set my Gaze on Alma and that crazy kid of hers and what happens?" Peyton's whiskers spasmed. "They never leave the building!"

Rebecca rolled her eyes and patted Peyton's head. Peyton had taken to blurting out the same sentiment at least every hour since the sun set over Emerald Tree Care.

"I can see them puttering about on the second floor," Rebecca said. "I don't think they're going anywhere. What do you think they're doing, and where's Jacob?"

"Who knows. This stakeout's turning into a real bummer. I was hoping for a car chase by now." Peyton wriggled her furry bottom and arched her head back. She looked up at Rebecca."I need to see a man about a carrot."

Rebecca chuckled and slowly opened the door.

"Don't wander off too far, you two. That's Forest Hills Park across the street. Believe it or not, it's over 500 acres of woods," The captain grumbled. "I'll take the next shift so you two can sleep, ok?"

"Jesus, you're always listening, aren't you?" Peyton asked.

Captain Wyatt smiled and closed his eyes.

Rebecca stepped out of the car and closed the door with her hip. She placed Peyton on the grass and let her hop forward to find some privacy.

After a moment, Peyton scampered back, jumped, and twisted her body in the cool night air. "So much better!"

Rebecca smiled, and turned her attention to the line of trees on their side of the street. Faint rays of white light squeezed between the trunks. "Come on, let's go see what that light's about. I'm sure Alma's not leaving anytime soon."

Peyton eyed the line of crowded trees. "Eh, why not."

They followed a dirt trail into the woods and emerged a few minutes later onto the outer edge of a little league baseball field. The chalk baselines glowed with an almost blue shimmer under the full moon's glare while six pole lights stood watch over the empty pitch like solemn sentries.

"It's beautiful," Rebecca said.

Peyton's back feet pounded the short-clipped grass. "Wanna race for home base?"

Rebecca nodded. "On the count of three, ok? One, two—" Rebecca snapped her head around and faced the woods. "Hey, is that a fox?"

Peyton gasped and flattened her body against the grass.

Rebecca laughed and bolted straight down centerfield toward second base. Her long, black hair trailed behind her like a battle pendant. She'd never beaten her partner in a footrace and hoped that this mean, but well-played trick would finally cement a win.

The sound of Peyton's feet thumping against the ground crushed all hope for a quick victory. Rebecca caught a glimpse of her partner's blurred form as she pulled ahead and dashed past the pitcher's mound.

In the blink of an eye, Peyton slid onto home plate.

Peyton hopped in a circle. "Undefeated!"

Rebecca stopped at second base, bent over, and clutched her knees. "Nicely done," she said, in between breaths.

Peyton shook her furry bottom. It was good seeing her partner so happy. Claire would have loved Peyton to pieces. Her little girl was so good with animals; the two of them would have gone on so many foul-mouthed adventures.

"Oh, yeah! Oh, yeah!" Peyton yelled, humping the air with one eye scrunched closed. Her whiskers bristled forward with each thrust.

Rebecca placed a palm over her face to block the vulgar scene.

Puffs of dirt bloomed by Rebecca's sneakers, snapping her out of her thoughts. Rebecca looked up at the cloudless night sky and wondered where the rain was coming from. She winced as something hard bounced off her forehead. A rivulet of blood oozed from the wound and snaked its way down her nose.

Peyton scurried toward Rebecca. "You're bleeding, Becca!" Peyton yelled, scurrying forward. She hopped around, sniffing the air. "Did someone just throw a pebble or something? I don't smell anyone around."

Rebecca dabbed the blood with her fingertips. "What the hell is—"

THUD!

Peyton and Rebecca screamed. A chunk of granite, the size of a window air conditioner, landed a few feet from the two inspectors.

Rebecca backed away from the huge rock, patting her chest.

"Are you ok, Peyton?" She didn't take her eyes off the granite. A thin dust cloud hovered over its jagged features.

Peyton scampered close behind, her breath wheezy and quick. She sounded like a dog's chew toy being pumped.

"Jesus Christ, Peyton! Answer me! Are you ok?"

Peyton spat a loogie toward the rock. "Yeah, sorry. I'm good!"

That's my classy partner, Rebecca thought.

A hail of pebbles peppered the field, sending the two running back toward the woods.

They crouched underneath the trees as the shower of rocks died down. Rebecca expected a chorus of crickets to follow, but nothing made a sound. The air was glacially still. A twig snapped somewhere in the darkness.

Peyton looked up at Rebecca. "Shit. Do you think the trees here are infected, too?"

Rebecca stood. Another branch snapped. She turned toward the sound. Two red eyes glowed within a rustling bush.

"Who's there?" Rebecca asked.

"*Hypnos!*" a voice shouted.

A cloud of tar-black ink exploded in front of Rebecca's eyes. Her head lolled backward and the muscles in her body relaxed so quickly that she thought that they turned into taffy. Rebecca crumpled onto the pine needle covered ground.

She wondered why anyone would shout out the God of Sleep's name in the middle of the woods?

Just before passing out, she heard Peyton squeal.

Chapter Nine
Hangover

Rebecca dreamed.

She wondered why she was lying on her back in the middle of the woods, but it was a dream after all. Her eyes focused on the pinpricks of starlight peeking through the dark canopy.

That's funny, I was just in the park, she thought.

A cool, evening breeze swept through the trees and tickled her goosefleshed skin. As the leaves rustled, the full moon, carried on a fluffy cloud the shape of a baby stroller, drifted into view.

Earth's lonely satellite popped out of the pram and plummeted through the atmosphere, shrinking in size as it hurtled toward her supine body.

Rebecca turned her head to the side and hoped the impact would be quick and painless. The killing blow never landed—the moon hovered an arm's length above her head.

"So cold," Rebecca whispered as freezing air radiated from the beach ball sized moon. She raised a hand and tapped the gray, pockmarked surface. *Bloop!* The moon jiggled like a water balloon and rotated half a turn.

Rebecca laughed as two enormous, brown eyes set within the moon's deep craters focused their attention on her. As they blinked, a jagged seam ran across the moon's surface like a jack-o'-lantern's crooked smile.

"Suarez? Can you hear me?" the moon asked.

Rebecca covered her face as a piercing white light bellowed from the moon's eyes.

"Inspector Suarez!" The moon yelled. Somewhere in the distance thunder cracked and her right cheek ached as if stung by a bee.

Rebecca bolted upright and shook her head. The captain, kneeling by her side, turned off the flashlight he was holding and placed a hand on her shoulder.

"Sorry about the slap. Are you ok?" he asked.

Rebecca rubbed her temples. "Jesus, someone used a sleep spell on me." She wobbled to a standing position. Her heart thumped against her chest. "Where's Peyton? Is she with you? Captain?"

Captain Wyatt stood and pursed his lips. "I sent Cole out to look for her. We thought she was with you. Do you remember what happened?"

"We were attacked on the ball field. Someone—"

"Attacked? How?"

"Someone started throwing rocks at us."

The captain's head jerked backward. "Rocks? Did some kids attack you?"

"No, this was magical. It *rained* rocks, Captain. It got so bad that we ran into the trees to find cover. That's when I blacked out." Rebecca raked her hands through her hair. "Oh, Christ. Someone took her. Someone took Peyton!"

"Calm down. We'll find her."

Rebecca turned as Cole skidded to a stop behind the captain.

"I looked everywhere. I can't find her," Cole said, fanning himself with his hat.

"I promise you that we'll find her," the captain said.

"Fucking right we will," Rebecca said, levitating into the air. Her blood-red leather jacket flapped in the breeze.

"Holy shit!" Cole shouted. "What are you doing?"

"Looking for clues," Rebecca said, waving her palms in a circle. "I can light up the leftover heat from any footprints on the ground."

Cole and Captain Wyatt stood mesmerized as the outlines of their previous steps slowly flared to life. Dozens of smaller impressions laid by squirrels, deer, opossums, dogs, cats, and raccoons appeared around the officers, flickering on and off like old neon lights.

"This is amazing," Cole said.

"How can you tell which ones belong to Peyton?" the captain asked.

As Rebecca's eyes rolled into the back of her head, a group of footprints by Cole's feet smoldered like freshly melted copper.

"That's her," Rebecca said, lowering herself to the ground. She kneeled to examine the bright-orange pattern. "She was here, right by my side, then she dashed off."

Rebecca raced alongside her partner's ghostly trail. Suddenly, a new set of human footprints, the color of lava, ignited behind Peyton's prints.

"Someone was chasing her," Rebecca yelled, dashing through the woods. A heartbeat later, she popped out a few feet away from the patrol car and watched as her partner's tracks evaporated.

She heard the Captain Wyatt and Cole approach.

"What happened? Did you lose the tracks?" the captain asked.

Rebecca shook her head and pointed at the red footprints snaking their way toward the arborist's building.

"Bastard took her in there." Rebecca was losing control again. Truly losing control. The magic inside her body boiled over and wriggled through her skin like a mass of fiery snakes.

Cole's eyes widened and bulged as a translucent crown of fire bloomed around Rebecca's head.

The captain grabbed Rebecca by the crook of her right arm. "Whoa, Suarez! We can't go in there with guns and spells blazing."

Rebecca pulled herself free and glared at the captain. Sparks of lightning arched between the spikes of her flaming headdress.

"At least let me call for some backup," the captain said, retreating toward the patrol car.

Rebecca narrowed her eyes. "Do what you have to do, but Peyton needs me. I'm going in there with or without you."

Chapter Ten
Snared

Peyton cursed herself for turning tail.

She couldn't help it. The dark figure that knocked Rebecca unconscious looked like a wolf-headed demon. When its eyes glowed red, instinct took over and Peyton dashed away.

She didn't make it far. Before she could hop into the police cruiser, the beast had somehow knocked her out. The last thing she remembered was being carried into the building by the ears.

She woke up inside a broom closet surrounded by cleaning supplies and the acrid smell of ammonia. It wasn't the most impressive of prisons, but the knob was too high for her to reach.

Peyton sniffed the doorframe. Cheap pine. She carved a lock picking rune into the doorframe with her claws. The wood peeled away like cucumber skin and pooled around her rear feet.

Peyton hopped back and admired her handiwork. Perfect. She closed her eyes and chanted, "*Éxodos, éxodos, éxodos.*"

The rune's jagged lines crackled with energy. As the light intensified, the lock clicked and the knob turned. Peyton pulled the door open with her front claws and slowly padded out into a large basement.

She was flanked by metal lockers on one side and cardboard boxes on the other. At the opposite end of the room was another door. Peyton took a step forward and froze as a strip of florescent lights flickered on and off.

The basement door slammed open and in walked her wolf-headed kidnapper, blowing bubbles from a plastic wand. Peyton scampered back into the broom closet. The creature followed; its clumsy footsteps slapped against the linoleum floor.

Peyton's fear flared into anger. She recognized those steps. She peeked out the door. This wasn't a demon! It was Alma's kid, Charlie, wearing a werewolf mask.

The boy stepped under the pale, blue light, and pulled off his disguise. He cocked his head to the side. "You got out."

"You!" Peyton growled. "Why did you do this to me?"

Charlie squatted. He dipped the wand into the plastic tube and blew a stream of bubbles into Peyton's face.

Peyton shook her head and sneezed.

"Because," Charlie said with no emotion.

The flatness of his voice chilled Peyton's blood.

"Because what?"

"Just because."

She wanted to curse and yell, but there was no point arguing a six-year-old. "Where's your dad, Charlie?"

"I put him to sleep in his office. You made him very sad today."

"What do you mean you put him to sleep?" Peyton asked. "You know what? That doesn't matter. You have to stop this. I need to—"

Charlie narrowed his wrinkled eyes and jerked his head forward. The ring of puffy fur that flared around Peyton's neck suddenly flattened as an invisible hand squeezed her throat.

The attack lifted her onto her hind legs and further into the closet. Peyton slashed at the air with her front feet as tears welled in her eyes.

"You made my daddy sad!" Charlie yelled as the overhead lights flickered.

Peyton's arms drooped to the side as black splotches clouded her vision. *This is it. This is how I clock out. Fuck!*

The force around her neck disappeared. Peyton fell to the floor and heaved in the musty air. She looked up and saw Alma hugging Charlie tightly.

"That stupid bunny wanted to hurt daddy," he cried, pointing a finger at Peyton.

Peyton shook her head. "That's not why we came. We'd never—"

Alma let go of Charlie. "It's ok, biscuit. It's ok. No one's going to hurt Daddy."

She walked into the broom closet and crossed her arms. "But we are going to hurt the bunny."

"Oh, fuck," Peyton gasped. "You can't touch me! It's a federal offense. You and your boy will go to jail!"

"No, we won't. Charlie here's going to make it look like you had a tiny heart attack." Alma pushed Charlie forward. "Just do it," she said.

Peyton's eyes widened as Charlie stabbed the air with two glowing fingers, drawing twin rivulets of red in the air.

"Alma! Charlie! Stop!" Jacob yelled as he entered the room. "What's going on here?"

The boy's fingers stopped glowing.

"Jacob! You're awake!" Alma turned to her son. "I thought he was asleep?"

Charlie shrugged his shoulders.

"Christ, this wasn't supposed to happen like this," Alma said, shaking her head. "No one was supposed to find out. *You* weren't supposed to find out!"

"Alma, what are you talking about?" Jacob asked.

Alma pointed at Peyton.

Jacob leaned his head into the broom closet. "Alma! That's the private investigator. She's *Loquizoa* for God's sake! It's a felony to harm one of them." He grabbed his wife by the shoulders. "Why are you doing this?"

"Because they came back. They've been spying on us. I'm sure they've sniffed out what we did—what I did," Alma said.

"Oh, God. What did you do?"

"I-I made Charlie—"

Alma looked up as the ceiling moaned and bowed downward. Cracks ran across the plaster, flaking off in large chunks.

Peyton scrambled under Alma's legs and hopped into an open metal locker as the family rubbed debris from their eyes.

Peyton exhaled. They didn't see her escape! They were more concerned with the collapsing ceiling. The last thing Peyton saw was Jacob, Alma, and Charlie running toward the exit and a flash of blue light.

Chapter Eleven
Rescue Mission

Rebecca didn't have time to pick a lock.

The glowing footprints she followed had slipped under Emerald Tree Care's locked, glass double doors. If she didn't get in soon, she'd lose the trail and any chance of finding Peyton.

She could wait for the captain or take matters into her own hands, risking her career in the process.

"Fuck it," she said, taking a few steps backward.

Rebecca steepled her hands over her nose and mouth and let out an ear-piercing shriek. The glass panels exploded into tiny shards and skittered against the wood floor. She stepped through the buckled door frame and followed the kidnapper's spectral footprints.

They led into the lobby before evaporating from view. Rebecca tried to raise the footprints again, but they refused to flare back to life. Whoever they belonged to didn't want to be found.

"Peyton? Peyton, can you hear me?" Rebecca screamed.

No one answered.

Rebecca hugged herself and paced back and forth. An image of Peyton's skinned body, hanging from a meat hook formed in her mind. Blood dripped from her partner's glistening, pink corpse and pattered against a wooden butcher's block.

Rebecca shook the thought away and stomped through the building, examining every room, kicking over furniture and overturning desks and tables. The frantic searching turned up nothing and led her back to the lobby.

She leaned against a wall and slowly slid down. She pounded her fists and feet on the floor. Peyton was gone and Rebecca blamed herself. It was her idea to explore the woods while Captain Wyatt and Cole slept.

Police sirens echoed in the distance. The backup Captain Wyatt promised was on its way. The shrill warble was of little comfort. Few suburban police departments had mages in their ranks.

If she was lucky, there'd be a Seeker, a mage specialized in finding missing persons, on call nearby.

A thin smile stretched across Rebecca's face as it dawned on her that she didn't need a Seeker. She already knew the basics of divination. She'd successfully closed a few missing persons cases with her rudimentary dowsing.

Rebecca reached into a coat pocket and pulled out a small brass cone attached to a leather cord. She stood and held the strap between her thumb and forefinger.

She pictured Peyton's round, furry face and constantly twitching nose. In response, the heavy pendulum rocked back and forth. It worked! Rebecca concentrated again and imagined Peyton frolicking in a grassy field.

The cone whirled in a wild ellipse, darting out of her grip, and lodging itself into the wood floor. The brass hummed as it burrowed deeper. *A basement. Of course. Peyton was somewhere in the basement.*

Rebecca's heart raced. Once again, the image of the blood-stained chopping block sprang into view. Peyton's flayed corpse wriggled and squelched on the thick wood.

Rebecca tried waving the image away, but her mind added a floating meat cleaver to the gruesome vision. The gleaming hatchet swooped down and cut Peyton in half. *Thunk!*

She braced her hands against the sight. Sparks ignited at her fingertips, singeing her skin. Rebecca shook her hands, painting streaks of light in the air.

Keep it together, Rebecca thought. *Don't let this turn into Kissena Boulevard.* If she let Hecate's Touch overwhelm her, the results would be disastrous, and this time there wouldn't be a demon to pin the blame on.

Rebecca exhaled in relief as the sparks faded. Her stomach gurgled and she doubled over in pain. It didn't work. Her magic, fueled by fear and anger, coursed through her nervous system like lava. A ball of heat erupted at the center of her body and flowed into her arms. Plumes of blue flames shot from her trembling, splayed hands. If she didn't release the magic, it would burn through her limbs.

The humming dowsing cone drew her attention. She aimed her trembling hands at its spinning base. Beams of blue plasma jetted out from her palms and blasted the floor.

The explosion knocked Rebecca onto her back. As the dust cleared, she crawled toward the edge of the freshly made crater. Acrid smoke curled from the jagged edges as filaments of bright, blue plasma continued to eat through the floorboards.

She flinched as the building's sprinkler system kicked on, bathing her and the room in sheets of cold water.

"No, no, no, no," Rebecca muttered, flipping her coat collar up. Too much energy had escaped. Had she obliterated her partner? She'd never forgive herself.

As the water died down, something moved in the darkness below.

"Peyton!" Rebecca yelled. "Are you down there?"

All she could hear was the sound of rubble settling into place. Then, a tiny cough.

"Peyton?"

"An energy blast? Woman, you used an energy blast? What were you thinking? You could have killed me!"

Thank the Goddess! Peyton was alive!

"Well, I didn't have much of a choice. You know how I get when I'm stressed out of my mind. You're welcome, by the way!" Rebecca leaned her head into the hole. "Who did this to you? Was it Alma?"

"No, it was Charlie."

"Damn. Then he's really a mage, isn't he?"

"Yeah, and I think—"

The sound of bare feet slapping on the wet floor turned Rebecca's attention. She shushed Peyton and stood. Someone was in the lobby with her. She turned and caught a brief glimpse of a small figure standing in the shadows.

"Charlie, is that you?" Rebecca asked.

A basketball-sized light ignited between the boy's hands. Rebecca's covered her nose as the smell of burning hair filled the air.

"What's going on up there?" Peyton shouted.

"It's—" Rebecca started to answer, but the strange orb discharged a stream of lightning, striking Rebecca in the chest and launching her out the lobby, through the shattered double doors, and onto the captain's parked police cruiser.

Chapter Twelve
Fight

Rebecca found herself staring at the night sky again. This time, it wasn't a dream.

A headache bloomed behind her eyes, her back ached, and every breath hurt. She cursed Captain Wyatt for driving an old Crown Victoria—the car's steel hood made for the worst possible landing pad. A hissing radiator and the car's shrill alarm warbled in her ears, adding to her misery.

Rebecca rolled off the buckled metal surface and landed on her hands and knees. Muffled shouts filled the air followed by frantic footsteps scraping over gravel.

Just as Rebecca was about to collapse, Captain Wyatt and Cole hooked their hands under her armpits and heaved her to a standing position.

Rebecca screamed—the sudden movement sent shockwaves of pain through her body.

"Get off!" Rebecca shrieked, slapping their hands away. She leaned against the car and let out a barrage of short breaths. "I think my ribs are busted."

Rebecca felt her sides with trembling fingertips and winced. "Yeah, something's broken or at least bruised to bits. It hurts to breathe."

"What the hell just happened?" Captain Wyatt asked.

"Alma's kid happened," Rebecca said, slowly buttoning her jacket.

The captain shook his head. "Charlie? He's that powerful?"

Rebecca nodded and reached for the captain's hand. "We're going to need that backup."

"Backup is almost here. I hope they're bringing a mage of their own," the captain said, helping Rebecca to stand.

Rebecca rolled her eyes. "What are the chances this suburban police department has a mage powerful enough to take on Charlie? He almost killed me, and I'm one of the strongest spell casters on the East Coast!"

"You're right," the captain said. He rubbed the stubble on his chin. "Can you heal yourself?"

"Yeah, but I'll need a few minutes." Rebecca winced from the pain.

"Guys, you're going to want to look at this," Cole said, pointing toward a column of light rising from Emerald Tree Care.

Rebecca turned to see an enormous phosphorescent plume shoot out the roof. Splintered timber frames, brick work, metal, and plaster rained down on the parking lot. Rebecca, Cole, and the captain sprinted across the street.

"Everyone ok?" Captain Wyatt asked.

"Peachy," Rebecca said, slapping dust off her shoulders. "You ok, Cole?"

Cole nodded and sat on his haunches. "What the hell—"

Another blast snapped their attention back toward the crumbling building. They watched Jacob and Alma dart from the entrance as fire flared from every window. The couple flattened themselves to the ground and covered their heads with their hands.

Rebecca rushed forward, but the captain held her back. He shook his head and pointed toward what was left of the roof. Charlie floated up from the rubble into the night sky holding Peyton by the ears. Her body dangled limp in the boy's hands.

Rebecca screamed, shattering the patrol car's windows.

Peyton squealed and struggled within Charlie's grip. The sound must have startled her. *She's alive!*

Rebecca's crown of fire sputtered back to life. Her anger boiled over, but this time she was focused, and concentrated all the energy into her right hand.

Strands of copper light swirled around her fist. She levitated into the air as the energy solidified into a long, basket-hilted sword. Rebecca pointed the fluorescent blade's tip at Charlie. "Give me back my friend, you little brat!"

Spectral skeletons faded into view behind Charlie's shoulders. The jade-colored ghosts, held together by stringy strips of muscle and flesh, moaned and swirled around his head. Their translucent forms tightened into concentric spirals that flowed into Charlie's ears.

Rebecca's bowels turned to mush.

He's a goddamn necromage!

Charlie's mouth opened so wide that Rebecca heard bones crack. Then a stream of thick, ectoplasmic bile jetted out from the boy's gaping maw.

Rebecca formed an energy shield in her left hand and braced for impact. The viscous, gruel-like stream undulated through the air with a screaming skull made from the roiling, tallow-colored slop at its head.

The liquid's impact forced Rebecca back to the ground, causing her feet to carve deep furrows in the grass as another round of bile pressed against the shield. The stench of rancid pork filled the air.

Rebecca anchored herself in place by driving the sword into the ground. Sprays of yellow ectoplasm bounced off in sizzling spurts. She held back the urge to vomit as it splattered on her coat and burned through the leather.

"Goddamnit, Charlie! I don't want to hurt you, but you're leaving me no choice!" Rebecca screamed, raising her sword.

Charlie snapped his mouth shut and formed a ball of lightning in his free hand. The wrinkles on his face deepened as if all the moisture in his skin suddenly evaporated. "Mom said I have to stop you—"

Gunshots rang out, and Charlie covered his ears with his hands, dropping Peyton into the flames below as Rebecca screamed.

"Stop!" The captain yelled, lowering his spent pistol. "No one is going to hurt anyone anymore."

"Peyton!" Rebecca screamed. Explosions bloomed on the side of the building as propane tanks and gasoline canisters ignited. A heat wave rippled from the ruins, extinguishing Rebecca's crown and sword. A second blast knocked Rebecca onto her back.

I'm too late. She caught a glimpse of a tall, blurry form as it rushed past her before her vision faded to black.

Chapter Thirteen
Revelations

Rebecca propped herself up on her elbows.

A high-pitched squeal rang between her ears. Her head swiveled in a slow, creaky arch. To her left, Captain Wyatt waddled in a circle, clutching his head; on her right, Cole crawled on all fours, retching onto the gravel; and straight ahead stood Alma, looking up at her floating son.

How the hell is she still standing?

They were talking. No, they were arguing. Alma screamed and pulled at her hair. Spit flew out of Charlie's mouth, but Rebecca couldn't understand what they were saying.

Slowly, the ringing in her ears faded and Alma's voice rose to the surface.

"It's over, Charlie! You have to stop all of this!" Alma shouted.

Charlie grasped his head with both hands. His hair had turned silver. "But you made me do this! Told me exactly what to do. You promised everything would be ok!"

"I didn't expect everything to go so wrong. No one was supposed to get hurt. . .or killed." Alma looked at her trembling hands. "Jesus, I asked you to kill that poor rabbit. What the hell was I thinking?"

Alma pointed at the crackling fire. "All of this is my fault. I wanted to save our family, but I just made everything worse. I should have never asked you to cast that incantation on those trees. I am so sorry."

A gust of hot wind dried Rebecca tears. There. They had solved the case. Alma and Charlie were the ones who created the killer trees in Flushing. But why? And what the hell was the point of the spell?

Charlie lowered himself to the ground and ran into his mother's arms. Alma stroked her son's head until he fell asleep. A faint light glowed from her fingertips.

Captain Wyatt rested a hand on Rebecca's shoulder and squeezed. "Are you ok?"

Rebecca slapped his hand away. "Peyton's gone!"

"No, she's not," Captain Wyatt said, jutting his chin toward the burning building. She turned in time to see a tall figure jogging out from the rubble. It was Jacob! He raced through the parking lot cradling Peyton in his long arms. Rebecca could see her head peeking out from the orange jumpsuit she was swaddled in.

Rebecca stood dumbfounded as Jacob unwrapped her partner. Peyton leaped into Rebecca's arms and scrambled up to her shoulders. She squeezed Peyton and twirled. The only other time she felt this happy, relieved, exhausted, and scared was when Claire was born.

She stopped and faced Jacob. "How? How you'd get to her?"

Jacob whispered, "I heard a voice. A woman's voice." He leaned closer. "She told me I had to rush into the building to save Peyton. Next thing I know, my legs are pumping and I'm running into that!" He gestured at the fire.

He coughed and wiped the sweat off his brow. "The fire. God it was awful. I felt like my skin was going to peel off, but it parted like a curtain for me. I ran straight through the opening and found Peyton lying on a pile of rubble."

Rebecca shook her head. "I don't understand—"

Jacob held his hands up and backed away. "I'm so sorry. I had no idea what Alma and Charlie were up to." He looked at Peyton. "If I'd known, I would have stopped them. At least tried to."

Before Rebecca could say anything else, Jacob jogged over to Alma and wrapped his long arms around his family.

Peyton coughed. "Isn't anyone going to ask how I'm doing? Oh, I'm fine. My ears hurt and I just fell a hundred feet into a burning building, but thanks for asking."

"How did you survive the fall?" Rebecca asked.

Peyton looked over to Charlie. "I think Charlie saved me," Peyton said. "He must have stopped my fall at the last minute. I remember him letting go of me, but that's about it. The next thing I know, I'm in Jacob's arms and bada bing, bada boom out we went."

"That's not possible. The kid was spooked by the captain's shots. He was frozen in place when he let you go."

Peyton narrowed her eyes. "Then someone else must have saved me."

Rebecca glanced around the lot. "Who the hell do we thank then?"

Chapter Fourteen

Radish

"**Y**ou can thank *us*," a voice purred.

Rebecca turned. A few feet away stood a hazy figure. The stranger's body was the color of charcoal and blurred in and out of focus.

The light from the crackling fire and oncoming sirens seemed to bend around the shape, keeping it in constant shadow. Whoever or whatever it was, toyed with a Zippo. The familiar click of the lighter's metal cover pinging open and closed echoed in the air.

The wick ignited, and a small, yellow flame revealed a round chin, a bulbous-tipped nose, and sensuous lips lacquered with the deepest, glossiest shade of red Rebecca had ever seen. The long cigarette pinched between the sensuous mouth flared to life.

"Who the hell are you?" Rebecca asked.

The figure snapped its fingers and the haze surrounding their body flaked off like old paint.

A tall, redheaded woman in a dark blue, pinstripe suit stepped forward. Framed within her flared shirt collar, a life-sized silver rabbit's foot charm on a thin, gold necklace bounced against her pale chest with every step.

The woman smiled as Cole stepped to the side like an embarrassed schoolboy. The rookie shuddered as she walked past, her snakeskin high heels crunching against the gravel.

She stopped in front of Rebecca and extended a slender hand. "Hello, I'm Radish."

The strange woman's grip was powerful, and her frigid skin and knobby fingers felt like they were carved from alabaster.

"I'm Rebecca Suarez, private occult investigator," she said, slipping out of the handshake and glancing down at down at Peyton. "And this oddly quiet *loquizoa* is my partner, Peyton Marx."

"It's a pleasure to meet you both," Radish said, taking a long drag. She blew the smoke out from the corner of her mouth. "I'm the head of talent acquisition at WITA, the Washington Irving Thaumaturgical Academy in Sleepy Hollow."

Was she Southern? Radish's accent was subtle, but honeyed, and hung in the air like the wisps of curlicued cigarette smoke collecting around her head.

Rebecca found herself staring for no reason. Peyton scrambled up and wrapped herself around Rebecca's neck like a fox fur scarf.

"What's gotten into you?" Rebecca asked.

"She's a *pneumazoa* host!" Peyton hissed.

Rebecca's eyes widened. "You're not a mage?"

Radish smiled and shook her head.

"I'm sorry. I just assumed that—"

"No offense taken. Folks always think I'm one." Radish stepped forward and placed a palm over the side of her mouth in mock whisper. "At least it's a step up from a limp wand."

Rebecca chuckled half-heartedly. *Pneumazoa* hosts were one of the least understood magical beings. The majority were older, male, and touched with only two skills—the ability to cloud their appearance and the power to channel the ghosts of dead *Loquizoa.*

The spirit animals hovered around their bodies, visible only to their host and living *Loquizoa.* Rebecca suspected there was more to their powers than they let on.

Radish flicked the cigarette butt toward the burning remains of Emerald Tree Care. "It's ok. You can ask me."

"No, no. I know that's rude. Your companion is—"

"A big fucking snake!" Peyton shouted.

Rebecca tapped her partner's nose. "I'm sorry. She has no filter."

Radish chuckled and extended an arm. "It's ok. Clive here is a Burmese python. Ten feet long and hard to offend. He says, *hello,* by the way."

Was the reptile coiled around her shoulders or slithering down her arm? Rebecca didn't know where to look, but Peyton's glare focused on Radish's fingertips, where presumably, Clive's head rested. Did she hear a hiss or was that her imagination?

"One day you'll have to tell me why *loquizoa* hate *pneumazoa* so much," Rebecca whispered.

"What are you doing here, lady?" Peyton blurted out.

"That's what I'd like to know," Captain Wyatt said. He'd been hovering close by with Cole at his side. "What business does WITA have here?"

The rookie held his hat over his belt buckle.

Radish tapped the embroidered crest on her suit jacket pocket. Inside the golden outline was the cruelest scene Rebecca had ever seen rendered in thread—a sleeping unicorn wrapped in silver chains. And below that, three Latin words stitched in red.

"*Colere et Fabricare*. What's that mean?" the captain asked.

"That's our academy's motto—Cultivate and Form."

Rebecca wrenched her eyes from the patch and looked at Radish. "What do you cultivate?"

"People mostly. Children like that young boy over there." Radish motioned toward Charlie cradled in his mother's arms. Jacob sat cross-legged in the grass nearby. The man looked like he'd aged a decade. "We'll be taking custody of Charlie, by the way."

Captain Wyatt laughed. "You don't have any authority to—"

"On the contrary," Radish said, unfolding a square sheet of paper. She handed the document to the captain. "That's a transfer order from the New York State Magic Officium cosigned by the governor *and* the NYPD commissioner giving my academy custody over this child."

Captain Wyatt stared at the order. Rebecca had never seemed him so pained. It was as if the words had assaulted him.

"How is this possible?" The captain grumbled.

"Our Sensitives predicted that we'd find a powerful mage in Forest Hills tonight. We filed our paperwork a few days ago and got here just in time to see the fireworks," Radish said. "You're lucky we did."

"You keep on saying *we*," Rebecca said. "But I don't see anyone else with you."

"Goodness! Where are my manners?" Radish said, stepping to the side. "This is my partner, Egon Muskrat."

What Rebecca thought was a patch of darkness was a Holland Lop Rabbit, as large as Peyton, but with jet-black, spiked fur. White spots peppered his snout and his clear, blue eyes sparkled as they met Rebecca's stare.

"I cushioned your partner's fall," Egon said.

"Thanks for that," Peyton said.

Egon bowed his head. "You're welcome."

"This is bullshit." Captain Wyatt folded the paper and slipped it into his front pocket. "People have died because of an incantation that boy's mother forced him to perform. We need to find out why they did it, who they worked with, and punish them."

Radish lit another cigarette. "I see. Egon, be a dear a bring the mother over. The captain here needs a bit of closure."

Egon stomped his rear right foot in Alma's direction, and her head jerked up and her arms went slack. Charlie rolled out of his mother's embrace and onto the grass. Jacob stood dumbfounded as his wife's body rose into the air and floated toward Egon. She came to a stop in front of the captain.

"Now, tell us what you did, and why," Egon said.

"I'm sorry," Alma whispered.

"I'm sure you are, but he needs to hear it," Egon said.

"Hear what?"

"Your confession!"

The captain stepped forward. "This isn't the right way to do this—"

Alma sobbed. Tears ran down her face. Her sudden outburst stopped the captain in his tracks.

"I just thought we could get away with it!" Alma blubbered. "Our business was going under. We have a mountain of debt and salaries to pay. God, do you know what the taxes are like out here?"

"I can imagine," Egon said. "Go on."

"I took Charlie on a pruning job in Flushing two weeks ago. No one on the crew knew what I was up to. I mean, how could they say no to the boss, right? So, I had them lift me and Charlie up on the cherry picker. That's when I asked him to place the spell—a simple skim job to make the trees absorb a little bit of cash from everyone that walked under them."

"How much money are we talking about?" Cole asked.

"Just a dollar or two from each passerby."

"Doesn't sound like much," Cole said.

"No, but we're talking about Flushing, Queens, one of the most heavily populated neighborhoods in New York City. I made over ten grand the first two days."

"It doesn't seem like you put all that cash to use. We noticed the sorry state of your building and equipment," Rebecca said.

Alma nodded. "The trees stopped giving up the cash."

"Why?" Rebecca asked.

"I have no idea. I thought the incantation had, you know, worn off. I was planning on taking Charlie back, but then you guys showed up today. I never meant—"

Egon shook his head, and Alma fell asleep. Her body rotated in the air like a balloon.

"There, that's a good start," Radish said. "I'm sure you'll have no trouble prosecuting Alma for this crime."

"You know, she also tried to get Charlie to kill me," Peyton said.

"See!" Radish beamed. "Another serious charge you can throw at her. Looks like this is a slam dunk case, Captain."

Radish walked forward. "Now, if you'll excuse us, we're going to collect Charlie."

"What are you going to do with him?" Rebecca asked.

"We're going to help him, inspector. The boy's clearly not in control. He's a danger to himself and others." Radish's eyes gleamed. "But there's so much potential. So much power that we can learn from and use. He'll fit right in with our stable of talented, young mages."

Rebecca's face twisted into a scowl. An image of the chained unicorn flashed in her mind.

To shape and form my ass!

Rebecca turned to the captain. "There's something wrong here. She's looking at Charlie like a lab rat. Couldn't we just call Child Protective Services?"

The captain shook his head. "No. Radish has authorization right from the top. When it comes to magical jurisdiction, the Officium has the final word."

"No hard feelings, Captain," Radish said. She marched past him and blew a kiss. "Oh, and just to show we're on the same side, Egon's already started wiping away Charlie's tree spell."

Rebecca watched Radish approach Jacob and Charlie with open arms with Egon at her side. "You know, this morning I thought the murderous trees were the worst thing about this case. But now I know that there's something far worse out there."

"What do we do about the human party decoration here?" Peyton asked, sniffing at Alma's feet.

"We bring her in," the captain said. "But we're going to need the cruiser's backseat. You two will have to take the subway home."

"That's just perfect," Rebecca said.

"Oh, and I'll need the two of you in my office first thing in the morning. We're going to have a little chat about you going rogue, Suarez."

"What did you do?" Peyton asked.

"I threatened Charlie. . .with my sword," Rebecca said.

Peyton laughed. "Well, I'm glad you didn't kill the kid, but the captain's either going to hold our pay or make us do some community service."

"Don't worry, you two will get paid," The captain said.

Rebecca groaned. "I hate community service."

Chapter Fifteen
Ride Home

Rebecca watched the Broadway station rumble past as their N train made its way toward Ditmar's Boulevard in Astoria. Peyton snacked on a granola bar next to her. The crumbs pattered against the hard, orange seat.

"Did the captain get back to you yet?" Peyton asked.

Rebecca unlocked her smartphone. "Yeah, he just sent a text."

"What's the body count?"

"Fifteen dead and ten maimed by the trees in Flushing," Rebecca said, tapping the screen. "Looks like Radish and Egon kept their word. The trees are clean now. There's no sign of Charlie's incantation."

Peyton burped. "Well, that's some good news. Alma and that crazy kid of hers sure did some damage. What do you think will happen to her?"

"I'm sure that she'll go away for a good stretch. She racked up a huge body count, and she did try to kill you."

"What about Charlie?"

Rebecca sighed. She stared at the crucifix-tipped white domes of St. Demetrios Greek Orthodox Cathedral as they sped by. "Who the hell knows. These academies are pretty secretive.

No one really knows what goes on in there and most are government funded."

Rebecca reached over and rubbed Peyton's head. "I just hope they treat Charlie well. The kid needs help."

Peyton nodded and looked out the window. "You know, there's still one thing I want to know."

Rebecca arched an eyebrow. "What's that?"

"I wonder if Egon's single?"

THE END

About the Author

Luis Paredes is a horror, fantasy, and weird fiction writer living in New York. When not crafting strange tales, you can find Luis tinkering with old typewriters or pursuing his other hobby—running.

Read more at https://luisparedeswrites.com.

About the Publisher

Platypus Book Press publishes speculative and weird fiction, horror, fantasy, crime, and sci-fi all under one strange roof.